THE DOG RULES

D0367278

A NEW PIG IN TOWN

Whether or not you like the smell of gym shorts
in the morning, you are sure to LOVE Coco
and Monty's first adventure:

THE DOG RULES

A NEW PIG IN TOWN

by Coco La Rue
illustrated by Kyla May

Scholastic Inc.

ISBN 978-0-545-46607-3

12 11 10 9 8 7 6 5 4 3 2 1   13 14 15 16 17 18/0

Printed in the U.S.A.   40
First printing, January 2013

Book design by Jennifer Rinaldi Windau

To Romayne,
a brave and beautiful bird
— C.L.R.

To all the dogs I love and have loved:
Max, Molly, Jed, Evie, Bambi, Mia,
Toby, Zoe, Gabby & Taylor
— K.M.

TABLE OF CONTENTS

Ask Abby
Avian* Advice for Our Fine Feathered Friends

Dear Abby,

I need advice. And, since I am no peacock, I am not too proud to ask for it.

Not too long ago I had a plan. Because I am a bird of superior intelligence, it was a very good plan. But it backfired. Instead of ridding my home of that mangy Monty, I was banished. My humans accused me of making "an unearthly racket" and said I would be kept out of the house until I stopped "screeching and squawking."

Abby, I do not like being banished. It is cold and damp in the garage. I cannot watch my favorite TV quiz shows. No one reads me bedtime stories.

What is a banished bird to do?

Yours,

Groveling in the Garage

*Avian: a fancy word for bird.

Dear Groveling in the Garage,

Your letter hurts my heart. It is sad to think that a fellow parrot has been banished!

First of all: Keep calm.
Second of all: Carry on!

If you are calm you will not screech and squawk. And if you can carry on being the brilliant bird that as a parrot you must be, your humans will notice, and return you to your proper roost.

As for Monty, try to look past his canine flaws. Befriend him so if things go south again, at least you'll be in the doghouse together! How bad can one dog be?

Best of luck,
Abby

Chapter 1

SINCE YOU'VE BEEN GONE

Dearest reader,
It is **wonderful** to see you again! You look fantastic! Rosy cheeks, sparkling eyes, and a bit of pep in your step! My, my, time has served you well.

It's true that when we last met I was in a bit of a bind, what with being banished to the garage and all. But no matter! Now I am a **better bird.**

Now I am **calm.**

Things have also changed for the Almost-Perfect Lane Family. If you'll remember, the Lanes would be totally perfect if they would just get rid of that dirty, disgusting dog, **Monty**.

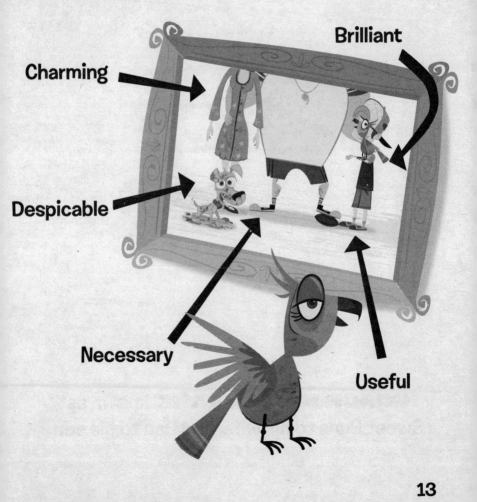

Brilliant

Charming

Despicable

Necessary

Useful

Remember the hairy head of the household? Well, Coach has moved on from his meat loaf infatuation. Now he is all about . . . the meatball! *

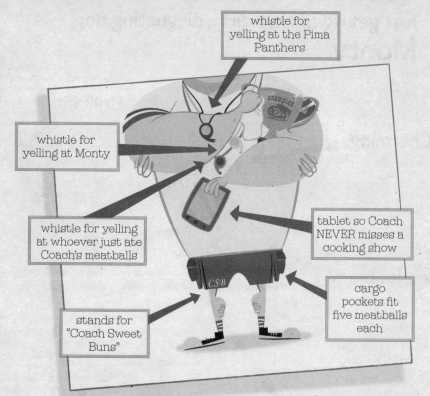

whistle for yelling at the Pima Panthers

whistle for yelling at Monty

whistle for yelling at whoever just ate Coach's meatballs

tablet so Coach NEVER misses a cooking show

cargo pockets fit five meatballs each

stands for "Coach Sweet Buns"

COACH WALKER LANE, known as Sweet Buns to his wife, and Dad to his son

* The small size makes it easier to keep that dog-tailed vulture from finding them!

As Pima County Hospital's new head surgeon, all Aurora wants to do is sew, sew, sew!* But the pressure of the job is getting to her. As Dear Abby would say, yoga helps her

keep calm and carry on!

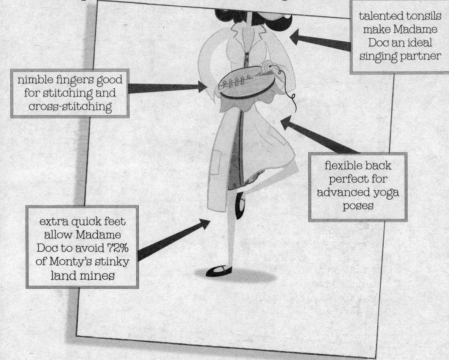

talented tonsils make Madame Doc an ideal singing partner

nimble fingers good for stitching and cross-stitching

flexible back perfect for advanced yoga poses

extra quick feet allow Madame Doc to avoid 72% of Monty's stinky land mines

Dr. Aurora Lane, henceforth
known as Madame Doc

* She has monogrammed Coach's gym shorts, Parker's socks ... and I suspect she is working on a monogrammed chess cape for me.

The pint-sized human has expanded his love of Star Wars to include all things space-related.

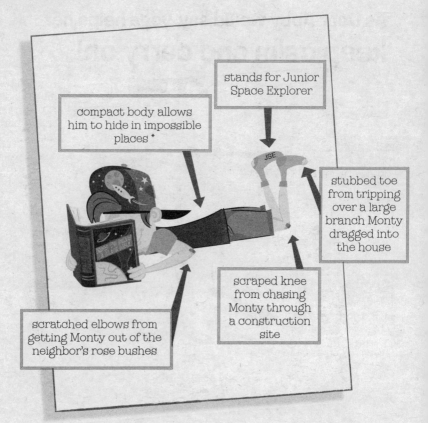

compact body allows him to hide in impossible places *

stands for Junior Space Explorer

stubbed toe from tripping over a large branch Monty dragged into the house

scratched elbows from getting Monty out of the neighbor's rose bushes

scraped knee from chasing Monty through a construction site

Parker Lane, Space Enthusiast

* Handy whenever it's time to mow the lawn or empty the dishwasher.

Most amazingly, Monty has taken up the harp! Every evening he serenades the family as we take a moonlit stroll around the pristine, dog-poop-free backyard ... **NOT!**

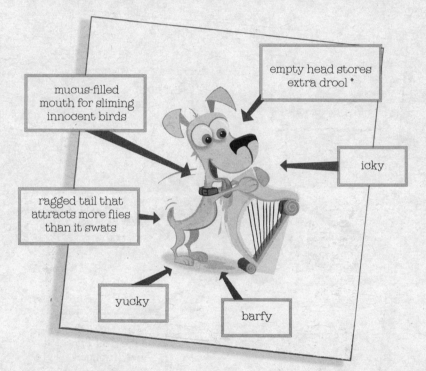

empty head stores extra drool *

mucus-filled mouth for sliming innocent birds

icky

ragged tail that attracts more flies than it swats

yucky

barfy

Monty, Mutt of Dubious Origin

* And not much else.

For me, the happiest change is that I am O-U-T of that awful garage. And, thanks to the advice of Dear Abby, I am a calmer bird. But, I am still the Coco you know and **love.**

brilliant brain that can solve any problem*

this bird's-eye view remains calm

heart full of peace and joy

notice my feathers are unruffled!

talons tapping to the beat of a new drummer

Coco LaRue, Parrot Extraordinaire

* Any problem except Monty, it seems.

Since we are being positive, let's not spend precious time rehashing unpleasant events. But before we move on, here is one last quiz about the tragic events of the past:

1. Coco wanted Monty, the Mutt of Dubious Origin, banished because he:
   A) always beats Coco at chess.
   B) makes fun of Coco's stuffy accent.
   C) smells like trash, gets away with everything, eats disgusting things, and about a trillion other reasons.

2. Coach threatened to send Monty to doggy jail if he:
   A) interrupted the Pima Panthers' football practice.
   B) ate Coco.
   C) ate Coach's meat loaf, ate Coach's gym shorts, played in the trash, or did anything else that's faintly doggy!

3. Which of these is Coco most likely to say?

    A) "Parker, can we get another pooch,
        pretty please?"

    B) "Monty, why don't the two of us spend
        the afternoon together?"

    C) "Shut your trap, you scallywag!"

4. Coco thinks parrots are the perfect pets because
they are most likely to:

    A) bake you a bird-shaped meat loaf.

    B) chew up your favorite pair of slippers.

    C) engage you in lively conversation.

5. Monty helped save the day by doing what
unlikely activity?

    A) Finding Madame Doc's wedding ring in a
        meat loaf.

    B) Rescuing Mr. Famous, the neighbor's cat,
        from a tree.

    C) UGH! Can you believe it? He did BOTH?

6. In the last book, who was actually banished?

    A) Monty.

    B) Coach.

    C) Coco LaRue.*

* Oh, the SHAME! It was ME! But MUST you rub it in?
Take pity on me, gentle reader. Pity, please!

If you answered mostly:

A's) Goodness, you dear thing—you are such an innocent! Such nice ideas about this cruel, cruel world we live in. If only life could be as sweet as you imagine! Sadly, you are WRONG!

B's) Yeegads! What a strange collection of answers to have chosen! Why on earth would Coach have been banished? He rules the roost! And to guess that Monty might have eaten me? How awful! Please, try again, for you are WRONG!

C's) As much as I hate to admit that some of these wretched things did happen, you are correct: They did. I don't know which is worse, the fact that instead of being banished, Monty was rewarded with bacon to eat and gym shorts to chew, or the fact that I suffered such shame.

But the past is behind us! Today I turn over a new leaf. I will follow Dear Abby's advice. I will stop trying to get that mongrel caught breaking Coach's Dog Rules. I will try to live in harmony with that stench pot. Instead of calling him the Mutt of Dubious Origin I will now refer to him by his real name: **Monty**.

Dear reader, I think I need you to wish me luck!

You're gonna need it!

Chapter 2

KEEP CALM AND CARRY ON

What's that, delicate reader? You're wondering how I followed Dear Abby's advice and became a calmer, less ruffled bird? By keeping a positive outlook on life, and always trying to find the cheery side of an **unpleasant, mangy mutt-filled** situation, that's how.

When a filthy dog shakes his mildew-infested coat, creating a horrid mud cloud all around you . . . look for the silver lining!

When a four-legged fart ball knocks over trash cans and litters the kitchen with banana peels and half-squeezed lemons . . . well, my little buttercup, simply make lemonade!*

* Or, in this case, batting practice.

To reach any goal, it is important to proceed step-by-step. Don't get overwhelmed, just work at your task one day at a time.

For the past few weeks, I've maintained a schedule that is sure to keep me calm and focused.

On Monday, Madame Doc and I practiced the ancient ritual of yoga together. We followed all the traditions:

We wore **yoga clothes.**

We **chanted.**

We listened to **calming nature sounds.**

We took **deep breaths.**

We drank **refreshing** water with slices of **hydrating** fruit.

Yoga has been practiced for more than 5,000 years, and millions of Americans enjoy its health benefits. I mainly like the poses named after **birds!**

crane pose

Crane you concentrate long enough do this pose?

eagle pose

This is an **eagle**-opportunity pose.

peacock pose

To do this meticulous pose, keep de tail down.

king pigeon pose

This pose is for the birds.

heron pose

Heron earth are you supposed
to get your leg like that?

Unfortunately, we neglected to wrap Monty in iron chains and lock him in the basement. Therefore, our yoga class was interrupted by **an unwelcome guest.**

Madame Doc needed a Boy Scout to untie that knot. We should have worn shower caps. **No matter! We stayed calm. We carried on.**

Ommm...Aiiiii

On Tuesday, Coach and I explored our culinary talents. What was on the menu? **Bacon-filled meatballs, of course!** With the help of Coach's new favorite show, *Cooking with the Colonel*, we chopped, we spiced, and we mixed. We baked, we sang, and we ate!

Famous Moments in

Most people know that meatballs are delicious, but only the brightest among us know that meatballs have served many important roles in history.

During the 1877 Moscow premiere of *Swan Lake*, the lead ballerina misplaced her tutu, and wore a skirt of meatballs in its place.

In an effort to save on electricity bills on the Statue of Liberty's 120th anniversary in 2006, officials replaced all light bulbs with 120 burning meatballs.

Meatball History*

Meatballs are frequently used to train Easter bunnies how to hide colorful eggs.

Before the lightweight Ping-Pong ball was invented, early players paddled meatballs back and forth over the net.

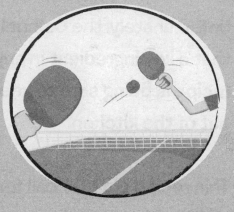

*Not to be confused with actual events in actual history that, you know ... actually happened.

Unfortunately, the Colonel did not mention that a key ingredient in any successful recipe is being sure to keep pesky pooches out of the kitchen.

This recipe did NOT call for a pint of slimy slobber. Or a cup of matted fur. Or a teaspoon of frolicking fleas.

DEEP BREATH!

It's OK, friendly reader, I am keeping calm!
I am carrying on!

Wednesday, Wednesday . . . What did I do
to keep calm on Wednesday? Oh yes, I
remember: art! The soothing, peaceful
act of painting. Parker and I worked on
family portraits.

Parker and I . . . had very

different artistic visions.

But once again, Monty ruined everything!

No artist could work this way! Michelangelo could have never finished the Sistine Chapel ceiling under these conditions! Being banished was better than this!

38

Chapter 3

WHY TEXT WHEN YOU CAN TELEGRAM?

DEEP, DEEP, **DEEP BREATH.**

Reader, I must tell you, **it isn't easy keeping calm in this atmosphere.** Not easy at all. Dear Abby, that great gray parrot, has given me some excellent advice to stay on course. But I am afraid this train is running off the track!

YELP
YELP
YELP

When a train runs off the track, a bird loses her cool. When a bird loses her cool, she starts to act a little berserk. And when a bird acts a little berserk, she gets **banished!**

SQUAWK!
SQUAWK!
SQUAWK!

Dear Abby's advice, while heartfelt, wise, and parrot-y, cannot help me here. I must consult a grand and miraculous oracle that has doled out pearls of wisdom through the ages.

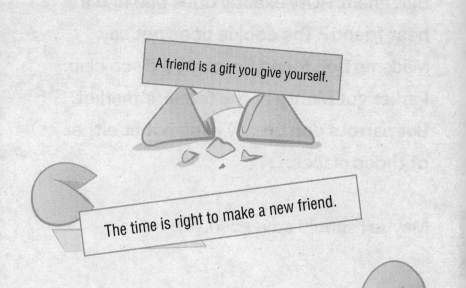

A friend is a gift you give yourself.

The time is right to make a new friend.

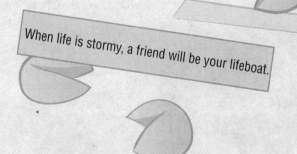

When life is stormy, a friend will be your lifeboat.

Aha! Thank you, clever cookies! Problem solved! I need a best friend to help me keep my cool!

But, ahem, HOW exactly does one find a best friend? The cookie does not say. Madame Doc found Coach at a disco club. Parker got Monty at the farmers' market. But parrots don't really hang out at either of those places. . . .

Maybe I should advertise. . . .

WANTED:
BEST FRIEND

Beautiful bird seeks best friend to provide support and advice. Experience un-ruffling feathers is a plus, but not required.

To apply, please contact Coco LaRue via carrier pigeon, snail mail, or pony express.

BEST-FRIEND APPLICATION

Dear Potential Best Friend,

Thank you for your interest in being my best friend. To see if we would be good companions, please answer the following questions:

1. What is your favorite hobby?
   A) Doing the crossword from *Birdbrained* magazine or trouncing an opponent in a game of chess.
   B) Skeet shooting and archery. If it moves, I can shoot it.
   C) Eating slop rules! Sleeping in a pile of trash is awesome! But nothing beats rubbing my hind quarters against a tree stump.

2. Do you like to sing?
   A) Why yes, I often croon in a chorus, serenade my sister, and sing in the shower.
   B) Sometimes I sing to lure my prey into a trap.
   C) Do you count howling at the full moon as singing?

3. What is your favorite kind of bird?

   A) The bird is such a superior creature that I must count the entire species as my favorite. But if you made me choose, the answer is clear: Parrots are breathtakingly beautiful and wildly smart.

   B) For eating? Anything covered in feathers tastes great.

   C) Bird ... bird ... what's that again?

If you answered mostly:

A's) Good gracious! You sound absolutely perfect! What skills! What composure! I think we would get along famously!

B's) Don't come any closer. I just called the police.

C's) I'm sorry, the position of annoying, stinky, stupid beast has already been filled.

This finding-a-friend business may take longer than I thought. Wouldn't it be nice if the mail carrier could just deliver one?

Ding-dong!

My goodness! Is that the doorbell? What a coincidence!

49

How thrilling!

A telegram!*

Telegrams are for VIPs and EIBs (Very Important People and **Extremely Important Birds**).

DEAR LANE FAMILY:

HAVING TEA BY THE SWAMP STOP WONDERFUL
WEATHER STOP JUST GOT YOU THE MOST
DELIGHTFUL PRESENT STOP WILL SEND STOP
LOVE,
GREAT-AUNT MILDRED

* You can recognize a telegram because it uses the word "stop" in place of a period at the end of a sentence.

Madame Doc's great-aunt Mildred (GAM) is a globetrotter, jet-setter, and trekker. In short: She travels. She loves to send notes and gifts from the strange and unusual places she visits. In fact, it was she who sent ME to the Lanes all those years ago.

Great-Aunt Mildred,
World Traveler

GAM is very generous. But if there were a punishment given for the strangest, most inappropriate gifts, she would probably get locked up in prison . . . on Mars. Just look at some of the gifts the old girl has sent over the years:

A membership in the Beet-of-the-Month Club from Poland.

A mock reindeer-antler hat from Alaska.

A three-foot-long
15th century
samurai sword
from Japan.

A set of
matching cuckoo
clocks from
Switzerland.

A collection of
designer paper
dolls from France.

However, the Lane Family isn't Almost Perfect for nothing. They come up with creative ways to use GAM's wacky gifts. For instance, the Lanes have:

redistributed them.

redecorated them.

re-gifted them.

repurposed them.

recycled
them.

LOVE,
GREAT-AUNT MILDRED
PS: THE PRESENT IS A PET!
PPS: NAMED PRISCILLA!

But, dear reader, today we are in luck! Just look at the postscript* on the telegram. What inspiring news! I almost hate to think it, but maybe—just maybe—this new gift of Great-Aunt Mildred's could be the very friend I've been searching for.

Priscilla the Parrot.

What fun we'll have together!

* A postscript is for forgetful folks who can't remember to write everything they want to all at once. A post-postscript is for those with the very worst memories. And a post-post-postscript . . . well, that's just lazy.

Chapter 4

PRISCILLA IN THE POST

The wondrous day has arrived!

Priscilla is here! Right now, at this very moment, we are about to open her crate.

Let's see, the box is a little roomy for a parrot, but perhaps that's just because Great-Aunt Mildred wanted to treat our bird with the proper respect. It's **strange** Great-Aunt Mildred didn't cut a hole for the beak, but maybe she didn't think of it.

I know, I know, **dear reader:** I shouldn't get my hopes up. It's true that **Priscilla** may not be a parrot. She could be a parakeet, peacock, or, goodness: a **pelican!**

OUR NEW PET HAS ARRIVED! PRISCILLA THE PONY!

The box is too small for a pony. But it's just the right height for Priscilla the penguin.

Peculiar!

Preposterous!

It seems I am not the only one with ideas about what kind of pet Priscilla might be.

Penguins don't live in the swamp! But Priscilla the porcupine might.

Perish the thought! Pfffft!

SQUEAL
ifyoulikemud

Arf!

Imagine our surprise when Priscilla the parrot turned out to be **Priscilla the potbellied pig!**

Goodness, gracious!

I'LL BE PICKLED WITH A PEPPER!

Cool!

Arf!

Squawk!*

* That is one strange bird!

Great-Aunt Mildred included everything we need to take care of Priscilla, plus a little something extra.

→ a change of hair ribbons

→ brush and comb

→ many, many frilly socks

→ special swamp treats for Priscilla

→ special swamp treats for the Lanes

Priscilla is an almost perfect companion.

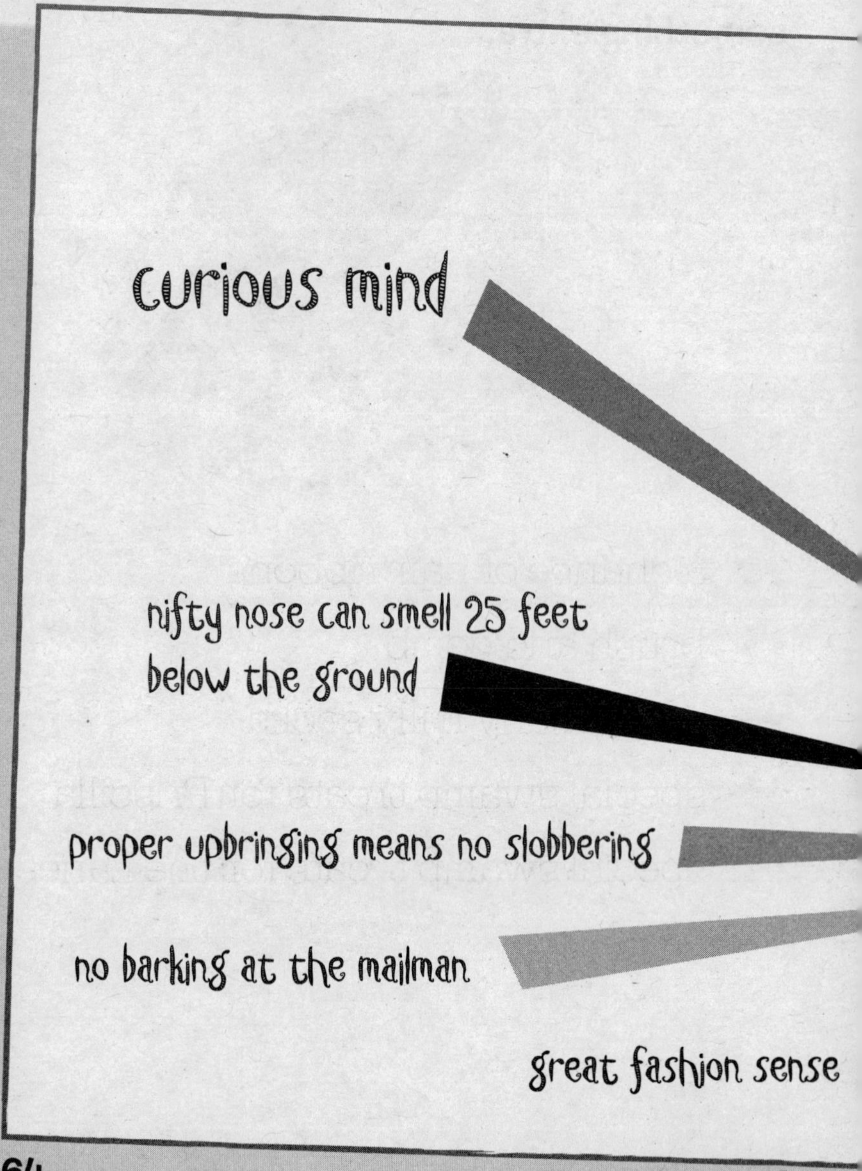

curious mind

nifty nose can smell 25 feet
below the ground

proper upbringing means no slobbering

no barking at the mailman

great fashion sense

soft, strawberry-scented hair
with absolutely NO fleas

cutesy-wutsey corkscrew tail
won't knock over lamps

Intelligence Quotient

Yes, pigs are wonderful. The list of their finer qualities goes on and on! But the most important is that **pigs are S-M-A-R-T**. After humans, pigs rank fourth in the smarts department. That's way ahead of you-know-whats.*

*dogs

Honorable reader, we are full of important questions about the new member of the household. We want her to be happy. We want her to be healthy.

What foods help a growing potbellied pig reach its ideal weight?

What educational toys help a pig reach its academic potential?

Do piglet TV stars grow up to be satisfied sows and boars?

Can you send your potbellied pig to market?

What type of mud is preferred for bathing?

But more importantly, can Priscilla carry a tune? Is she an alto or soprano? Does she have a talent for musical theater? In short:

Does she like to sing?

YES!

Does Priscilla know what a touchdown is? Is she better at playing half back or full back? Can she tell the difference between Coach's pigskin and her own? In short: **Does she like football?**

YES!

Does Priscilla have an insane desire to run around in circles? Is she tireless in her pursuit of an unreachable goal? Do whiskers and a gentle purr make her giddy? In short:

Does she like chasing cats?

YES!

Does she like mind games? Does she prefer to use brains over brawn? Will she be a worthy opponent? In short: **Does she like chess?**

YES!

Reader, Priscilla is just what the Lane family needed! She is buddies with the beast, chums with Coach, pals with Parker, and mates with Madame Doc.

And as for me? She is the stink to my cheese, the peanut butter to my jelly, the very best friend I've ever had.

We love Priscilla the potbellied pig!

Chapter 5

DIDN'T YOU READ THE INSTRUCTIONS?!

But of course, **the Almost-Perfect Lane Family** did not exactly live happily ever after. They are only **ALMOST** perfect, after all.

Smartest of all readers, you know how you are **ALWAYS** supposed to read the instructions before taking a test, using a new phone, putting together a LEGO model of the *Millennium Falcon*, knitting a sweater, flying a plane, performing a brain transplant, and **ESPECIALLY** BEFORE TAKING OWNERSHIP OF A FLORIDA-RAISED **POTBELLIED PIG?!?**

Way back on the bottom of page 63, did you happen to notice an envelope marked **"Special Pig Instructions"?**

The members of the Lane family—including yours truly—did not. **For shame!**

WHEN GOOD INSTRUCTIONS GO UNFOLLOWED
OR, NICE WAY TO TREAT GAM'S PRESENT, BUB:

INSTRUCTION: Brush Priscilla's hair 100 times before bed.
NUMBER OF TIMES HAIR WAS BRUSHED: 0
RESULT: Pig dreadlocks.

INSTRUCTION: Wash imported frilly socks by hand.
HOW SOCKS WERE WASHED: By sock-eating washing machine.
RESULT: All that's left is a pile of thread and one heel.

INSTRUCTION: Practice pig Latin for ten minutes every day.
NUMBER OF MINUTES PER DAY PIG LATIN WAS PRACTICED: 0
RESULT: Priscilla can no longer travel to ancient Rome.

INSTRUCTION THAT WAS FOLLOWED:
Give Priscilla one swamp treat per day.

INSTRUCTION THAT WASN'T REALLY AN INSTRUCTION
THAT WAS FOLLOWED:
Give humans one swamp treat per day.

Friends, followers, humans, pets, I simply cannot stress enough how important it is to read the instructions. **Look what happens when you do not follow directions when . . .**

knitting a sweater.

performing a brain transplant.

flying a plane.

changing a
baby's diaper.

baking
a cake.

Without following instructions to a T, the world goes crazy! Who knows what kind of trouble we have gotten ourselves into by missing that teensy-weensy envelope. The only one who noticed it was that rascally rogue Monty.

Chapter 6

SOMETHING STRANGE IS AFOOT

Beloved reader, insanity has taken over the family! What an odd week we've had here at the Lane household.

On **Monday,** Madame Doc and I did not meditate in flamingo pose. Instead, she changed our former yoga room into a **mud pit!**

84

85

On **Tuesday**, Coach's cooking channel was silent. Instead he emptied the fridge of all his beloved breakfast meats. **Good-bye, bacon! Good-bye, ham!**

On **Wednesday,** instead of drawing pictures
of Jupiter and the Milky Way, Parker was
obsessed with pictures of wolves, and houses
build out of **straw, sticks, and bricks!**

What has happened to the Almost-Perfect Lane Family? Why have they abandoned their usual hobbies? **Why has Madame Doc sewn little piggy tails on the back of everyone's pants?**

Why is Coach inviting fruit flies into the house? I obviously can't ask that dingbat Monty for help with this problem. Thank goodness Priscilla is here. Thank goodness Priscilla is smart and kind and clean and . . .

Eeeekkkk!

What is going on around here?!?

My precious pal Priscilla has gone **wackadoodle**, too!

Reader, we must remain calm. We cannot panic. We cannot fly around in a tizzy and pass out. And if, by chance, we do, we cannot hold it against one another! These are trying times.

Keep calm!
Carry on!

Let's take a moment to examine the situation:

→ Something is wrong with Madame Doc.

→ Something is wrong with Coach Lane.

→ Something is wrong with Parker.

→ Something is wrong with Priscilla.

→ I, Coco, am in perfect health.

Is there anyone left to examine?

Anyone?

Oh, right. Well, if I must, I must.

Everything looks normal here.

Chapter 7

YOU PUT A SPELL ON ME

Dear reader, since everyone else is acting oddly, we must take stock and make certain that our very own brains are in tip-top condition.

DID SOMEONE PUT A SPELL ON YOU?

→ Did someone in a silk robe covered in stars wave their fingers in front of your eyes while chanting the alphabet backward?

→ Did someone with a long beard and bushy eyebrows wiggle their fingers in front of your eyes while saying every other word from the Pledge of Allegiance?

→ Did someone with a black hat and warty nose give you a cup of tea made from a tin labeled "Eye of Newt" and then laugh wickedly when you drank the entire mug?

→ Do you have trouble remembering where the time has gone or what you've been doing?

→ Are your eyes swirly and unfocused?

If you answered "Yes" to more than two of the questions ...

you are in deep trouble, my friend.

If Madame Doc is spending all of her free time in a mud puddle, who will renew my subscription to *Birdbrained* magazine? If Coach continues with his anti-pork campaign, who will refill my food bowl? If Parker is keeping watch for trespassing wolves, who will tuck me in at night?

But most importantly, if sweet, smart, and sophisticated Priscilla stays zombified, who'll save me from a lifetime with only a rude, crude canine for companionship?

I have no choice. Despite my considerable brainpower, I cannot solve this problem on my own. I'll need that mischievous mongrel Monty to help me fix this mess. We have to brainstorm. **We have to plan. We have to help the Lanes!**

Monty, are you with me?

Dear reader, we must again review the facts:

A few weeks ago, I was making meatballs with Coach.

Then Priscilla arrived.

Then everyone started acting strange.

GASP! Could it be that our precious Priscilla is the cause of all of our troubles? Did her oinking cast a strange spell on the Lanes? Did her long eyelashes flap in hypnotic rhythm? Did her cutesy-wutsey tail mesmerize my family? And why didn't it work on Monty?*

* Of course, I am far too intelligent to ever fall for something like that.

Once again, I need advice. I need to hear from someone smarter than Dear Abby and wiser than a fortune cookie.

Oh, Magic Ball of Answers, has our new porcine pet, Priscilla, cast a spell over everyone?

Don't count
on it.

I have a plan. We will call Great-Aunt Mildred
and ask her specific questions about
Priscilla. GAM will know the answers.

Monty, are you with me?

GAM, Coco here. Monty and I have a few questions for you.

One: Is there anything **evil** about Priscilla's eyes?

Two: Is there anything **monstrous** about Priscilla's mouth?

Three: Is there anything **terrible** about Priscilla's tail?

Well, hello.
Nope.
Nuh-uh.
Not a thing. But that reminds me, I should send the Lanes another telegram about those swamp treats.

TELEGRAM

DEAR LANE FAMILY:

HAVING CRUMPETS BY THE SWAMP STOP

DELIGHTFUL SCENERY STOP GORGEOUS

GATORS EVERYWHERE STOP FORGOT TO

TELL YOU ONE THING STOP PIG TREATS

WILL CAUSE CRAZINESS IN HUMANS STOP

AND VICE VERSA STOP TREAT WITH A

TABLESPOON OF HONEY STOP

LOVE,
GREAT-AUNT MILDRED

Chapter 8

WHAT NEXT?

Dear reader, what do you think became of the spellbound Lane family? Did Coach swear off meat forever?

Did **Madame Doc** host mud-wrestling parties in the living room?

Did **Parker** sneak the pig swamp treats to school on test days?

Did **Priscilla** hitchhike back to Florida to swim with the skeeters?

Did Great-Aunt Mildred, the world traveler, get banished for sending such dangerous treats?

118

Did the Lanes finally send Monty away once and for all?

And what became of me, beloved reader?

Did my **feathers** ever **recover**
from this madness?

Did I start an **advice column**
of my own?

Did I pack my bags and move
to a **bird sanctuary?**

Did I start another **campaign**
to get **rid** of **Monty?**

Did I **travel the world** helping
zombified families?

Did the story of my **bravery** get
made into **a movie?**

Chapter 9

ALL'S WELL THAT ENDS WELL

Oh, reader, don't be silly! None of those
preposterous things happened. What kind
of crazy book do you take this for?

We followed the instructions in GAM's
telegram and gave the Lanes and Priscilla
a tablespoon of honey each.

And just like that, everything returned to Lane-family normal. Madame Doc resumed her yoga practice. Coach headed back to cooking with the Colonel. And Parker took up his paints.

As for the furry, feathered, and snouted in this animal house . . . well, take a look!

Yes, yes, we all lived happily ever after . . .

...that is, until the day we got another unexpected package from **Great-Aunt Mildred...**